HOW TO ACE COMPETITIVE EXAMS

R.Kesavamurthi

How to ace competitive exams

First Edition : November 2022
Pages: 66
ISBN : 978-93-5533-609-5
Aelay Publish
Contact : +91 9944992571
Designed by : Aelay publish team

CONTENTS

1. KNOW THE EXAM

PURPOSE

Competitive exams are conducted for one of the following purposes.

1. For selection of candidates for government and private jobs
2. For admission into graduate and post graduate courses
3. For getting scholarship from both State and Central government

EXAM TYPES

Recruitment Exams :

TNPSC Group Exams- Group 1 to 8, CDS (Combined Defence Services), CAPF (Central Armed Police Forces), IES (Indian Engineering Services), ESE (Engineering Services), NDA (National Defense Academy), UPSC Exams (Civil Services - Popularly known as IAS Exam), SSC Exam, Bank Exams, CBI etc.

Entrance Exams :

JEE, NEET, CLAT, NATA, ICAR, GRE, GMAT, GATE, CAT, TANCET, MAT etc.

Scholarship Exams :

NMMS, TRUST, NTSE, KVPY, OLYMPIADS, TTSE etc

MODE

Objective type questions with multiple choice answer options. One question shall have 4 or 5 answer options, out of which one is the correct or the most appropriate answer. If it is Pen and Paper mode, an OMR sheet will be given which is to be filled by the candidates. Oval shaped circle in the OMR sheet is to be darkened completely without gap. If it is a computer based exam, a tick is marked in the given OMR format. There are two types of computer based exam.

1. Examinee shall go to a specified computer lab and write the exam
2. Proctored computer based exam from home

LEVEL OF COMPETITION

One gets selected out of 200 or 500 candidates appearing for the exam. Examiner aims to reject as many candidates as possible by giving the following types of questions:-

Difficult questions	Time consuming questions
Confusing questions	Misleading questions
Twisted questions	Providing irrelevant data in the question

DURATION

Most of exams have duration from 2 to 3 hours. Accordingly the number of questions may vary. On an average one minute is available for answering one question.

TYPES OF QUESTIONS

1. Quantitative Ability

2. Reasoning - Diagrammatic Reasoning, Logical reasoning - using diagrams, scenarios,shapes & imagery, Numerical Reasoning – through simple problems, Verbal Reasoning – to assess verbal logic, Inductive Reasoning – to see patterns and analyse given data, Abstract Reasoning – to assess general knowledge, and ability to utilise knowledge in new situations.

3. Situational Judgment – Tests problem-solving ability

4. Data Interpretation

PATTERN OF QUESTIONS

The aptitude test may comprise questions of Multiple Choice type (MCQ), Multiple Select type (MSQ), Preferential Choice type (PCQ) and Numerical Answer type (NAQ) and Match the following type (MFQ)

EVALUATION PATTERN

These exams have 3/4 marks for right answer. Most of the exams have negative marks ranging from $1/4^{th}$ to $1/3^{rd}$ of the marks for the correct answer. For unanswered question negative marks is not applicable.

VALIDITY

The score obtained in these competitive exams is valid for specific duration or time or purpose. Validity for the jobs or recruitment tests is specified in that notification. Exam to get admission is valid for one or two or more years. Exam for scholarships is valid only for that specific year.

RESULTS, QUALIFYING MARKS AND CUT OFF

Results are declared within 2-3 months from the time of writing the exam. Result includes absolute marks for each section of the question paper and also the cumulative score. It also specifies the percentile score. For example 90 percentile means that 90% of the candidates obtained lesser score than that candidate.

HOW & WHEN TO APPLY

Most of the exams have on line application. Candidates have to fill the application form and then, upload necessary documents for id and address proof, proof of community the candidate belong to, OBC certificate, age proof, mark or grade sheets.

2.0 <u>STUDY THE SYLLABUS</u>

Syllabus is provided along with the notification for the exam. Level or standard of the exam is also indicated in the notification. For example – school final level or graduation level etc.

Course Material : Based on the portions or chapters or topics identify source of materials for each chapter. Understand weightage of marks for each section.

<u>COMMON TEST AREAS OR SECTIONS</u>

Some common test areas are given below:

<u>MENTAL ABILITY TEST</u>

The mental aptitude test problems, sometimes called Aptitude problems, test the reasoning & interpretation skills of candidates. This is done by looking at how a candidate approaches problems of the test. There is not an established theory to it. However, over the years, mental ability test has moulded itself into a set of questions which are still growing in variety. The best part is that the questions that can be asked in a mental ability test are growing in variety faster than the theory of science or commerce.

Mental ability areas include:

Direction sense, blood relationship, number series and analogies, letter series and analogies, verbal analogies, deductions, venn diagrams, mirror image, water image, clocks, calendar, cubes, coding and decoding, missing numbers, logical reasoning, counting of squares and rectangles etc

GENERAL STUDIES

General knowledge questions are from history, geography, science, civics, economics, sports, politics etc. School level subjects books are source of materials for this section. In addition to this regular reading of newspaper and weekly are recommended

BASIC MATHS / QUANTITATIVE

Math's syllabus includes math's areas up to 10th standard level. They include time and work, time and distance, percentage, ratio proportion, simple and compound interest, geometry and mensuration, numbers, arithmetic and geometric progression, permutation and combination, probability, statistics, inequalities, simple equations, indices, averages and mixtures, quadratic equations etc.

DATA INTERPRETATION

Tables, Graphs, Pie Charts, Bar Charts are given and questions are asked to assess the interpretation ability of the given data. The questions will require to derive, infer, and manipulate numerical information set out in such passages, graphs, or other representations; and apply various 10th standard mathematical operations on such information, including from areas such as ratios and proportions, basic algebra, mensuration and statistical estimation.

DATA SUFFICIENCY

To assess whether the given data or information is sufficient to arrive at the given conclusion

BUSINESS JUDGEMENT

In a given business situation candidates are asked to find the major objective, minor objective, major assumption and minor assumption

CURRENT AFFAIRS AND GENERAL KNOWLEDGE

Questions that will require to demonstrate the awareness of various aspects of current affairs and general knowledge, including contemporary events of significance from India and the world, arts and culture; International affairs; and historical events of continuing significance.

READING COMPREHENSION

In this section, you will be expected to read passages. The passages may relate to fact situations or scenarios. Each passage would be followed by a series of questions that will require you to answer.

TAMIL LANGUAGE

TNPSC Exams include questions from Tamil Grammar, Tamil Literature and Tamil Scholars and their writings.

3.0 <u>PLAN THE PREPARATION</u>

Study plan
Study Time
Routine & Networking
Mock Tests, Gap Anlaysis, Error Analysis and Past Question Papers

<u>STUDY PLAN</u>

Have a plan to use the time ; such as study time, revision time, test taking time, checking answers and solutions etc. Take one day at a time. Decide on three things you want to do for that day. Write a diary on what comes to your mind. Do peer learning. Support each other. Take stock of the activities once a week, do not bother about the things which are not in your control such as marks, grades, all india rankings, scores etc. Instead plan about things that are in your control.

<u>THINGS THAT ARE IN YOUR CONTROL</u>

1. PREPARATION
2. ATTITUDE
3. TIME MANAGEMENT
4. PRIORITY
5. EXPECTATIONS
6. NETWORKING

<u>**STUDY TIME**</u>

Be calm and do not be nervous and learn to manage yourself. Then you manage writing exam. Study for about say 30-40 minutes and take a break of about 10 minutes. Recall and revise. Attempt writing test and check for solutions. Study for 3 hours per day consistently for 2 years (say 2 hours of coaching and one hour self study)

<u>**ROUTINE**</u>

Do not become addict to mobile or computer games. Have schedule for mobile phone usage or social media interactions

SOME TIPS ARE :

1. Keep your mobile phone in some other room in the night.
2. Have schedule for sleep and try to follow
3. Put extra effort every day in areas of your shortcomings
4. In the morning do not checkup phone for at-least first 30 minutes

how to ace competitive exams

ATTITUDE

There is a dearth for attitude. There is no competition for attitude. Do not feel bad about you. Be kind to yourself, mom and other family members. Take scheduled breaks and do other things.

LOOK AT THE FOLLOWING:

- What you can do for yourself
- What you can do for your family
- What you can do for the community

MOCK EXAM, MODEL TEST PAPERS

MOCK Exam and model test papers are vital in the preparation. Students on a regular basis must subject themselves to mock test papers. This shall help in two ways viz gap analysis, error analysis

GAP ANALYSIS

Identify gap in the preparation. Chapters which are weak in or chapters where the concepts are not clear etc. can be identified by doing gap analysis. This shall enable the student to go through those portions and study again on own or in consultation with teachers or mentors. This step has to be repeated till the time student covers all the portions given in the syllabus

ERROR ANALYSIS

Students have to do an analysis of the incorrect answers. Reasons for not getting the correct answers have to be understood.

Broadly, it could be due to one of the following reasons.

1. Not thorough with that portion of the subject. Clarify the doubts with teachers or mentors or through you tube videos. Can go through books other than board books viz NCERT / State Board books.

2. Question is confusing

3. Misunderstood the question

4. Numbers or Figures are used wrongly

5. Silly mistakes

6. Time not sufficient and hence in hurry

4.0 <u>EXAM STRATEGY</u>

<u>READING THE QUESTIONS</u>

Read each question twice before answering. Even if it is clear for the first time, read it for the second time. If question is not clear after reading for the second time, skip and move to next question Read all the questions during that exam duration. You need not attempt all the questions. Last 20 - 30 questions may be much easier.

<u>ATTEMPTING THE QUESTIONS</u>

Each question is given about 1 minute to answer. If you consume more than say 2 minutes then we can safely say that the methodology followed is wrong.

Attempt as many as questions as possible. In the exam read through all the questions. Need not attempt all. Attempt questions known to you. Put a dot on questions which you have understood, but could not get the answer, so that you can come back at the fag end

<u>SECTIONS AND STOCK TAKING</u>

Attempt more questions on sections which are easier in the exam on the given day. A particular section is easy for a candidate so he or she plans to maximise the score in that section. But it may so happen that in the exam some other section may come easy, so attempt more questions in section which is easy in that paper.

Every 30 minutes, do a stock taking of number of questions attempted. Get up from the seat and do some physical movement so that monotony can be broken.

METHODS OF ANSWERING
ELIMINATION METHOD

Q: WHICH IS BIGGER ?   4/5 2) 5/7 3) 7/9 4) 6/7

In these questions there are 4 options. The difference between numerator and denominator is one in two options (1 & 4) and 2 in other two options (2 & 3). So obviously answer can be one of the options which has difference 1. Among those options calculate the value: Option 1 value is 0.8 and Option 4 value is 0.85. Answer is Option 4

SUBSTITUTION METHOD

Q: Ramesh has 30 coins consisting of 10np and 25np. If the total is Rs 6, how many of each variety does he have
1) 15,15   2) 20,10   3) 10,20   4) none of these
Substitute option 2 and the value is
(10 x 20 + 25 x 10) = Rs 4.5

This value is less than the total Rs 6/-. So we need to go to option where the number of 25 np coins are more than 10. So go for substitution of option 3 and the value is
(10x10 + 25x20) = Rs 6

METHOD WITHOUT FORMULA

Q: At what angle (in degrees) are the hands inclined at 50 minutes past 8 ?
1)55   2) 35   3) 22.5   4) 60

Visualise the clock and the time. The hour hand is between 8 and 9 and minute hand is pointing 10. So the angle is more than 30 but less than 45. So Option 2 is the answer.

METHOD WITH FORMULA

What is the simple interest for 20 months @10% interest per annum for a sum of Rs 1000/- Formula for Simple Interest (SI) is = PNR / 100 SI = 1000 x 20/12 x 10/100= Rs 166.66

Here N must be written in years and hence N= 20/12

TIME MANAGEMENT

Read each question twice before answering. Even if it is clear for the first time, read it for the second time. If question is not clear after reading for the second time, skip and move to next question.

Read all the questions during that exam duration. You need not attempt all the questions. Last 20-30 questions may be much easier.

SPEED

Each question is given about 1 minute to answer. If you consume more than 2 minutes then we can safley say that the methodology followed is wrong. Attempt as many as questions as possible. In the exam read through all the questions . Need not attempt all. Attempt questions known to you. Put a dot on questions which you have understood, but could not get the answer, so that you can come back at the fag end.

MAXIMISING SCORE

Attempt more questions on sections which are easier in the exam on the given day . A particular section is easy for a candidate so he or she plans to maximise the score in that section. Buy it may so happen that in the exam some other section may come easy. So attempt more questions in section which is easy in that paper. Every 30 minutes, do a stock taking of number of questions attempted. Get up from the seat and do some physical movement so that monotony can be broken

NEGATIVE MARKS AND RISK

Suppose you guess 10 questions, then if 3 are correct and 7 are wrong, then gain is 2 marks. If 2 are correct then loss is 1. If 4 are correct then gain is 6 marks.

Possible 3 scenarios in the last 10 minutes

SCENARIO 1: ATTEMPTED 80 /100 AND 60 ARE CORRECT.
SCORE IS : 240 – 20 = 220   ACTION - ATTEMPT MAX 5

SCENARIO 2: ATTEMPTED 60/100 AND 50 ARE CORRECT.
SCORE IS : 200 – 10 = 190   ACTION - ATTEMPT 10 MORE

SCENARIO 3: ATTEMPTE D 50/100 AND 45 ARE CORRECT.
SCORE IS : 180 – 5 = 175   ACTION - ATTEMPT 15 MORE

5.0 <u>DOs AND DONTs</u>

1. Go to the exam center well in advance. If it is a new place/town, then go to that town the previous day.

2. Take all the necessary items such as admit card, pens etc.

3. Go to the toilet before entering the exam hall

4. Eat well before going to the exam hall

5. Flip through the question paper booklet and make sure all the papers are printed and there is no blank sheets inside

6. Write the roll number as given in the admit card

7. As soon as exam starts, glance through the entire paper to get a feel on the difficulty level

8. Start answering questions which is known to you.

9. No question requires more than say 2 minutes to answer. If you consume more than 2 minutes to answer any question, then your methodology could be wrong. Do not waste time on any one question.

10. Every half an hour or 45 minutes, take a physical break like standing for a moment

<u>GRATITUDE : SAY THANKS</u>

Thank your parents and family members
Thank your teachers and seniors / fellow students

<u>NEVER NEVER GIVE UP</u>

Getting lower marks is not a crime
Life is beyond studies and marks
Never give up in studies / career / life

6.0 <u>WHAT TOPPERS HAVE TO SAY ABOUT PREPARATION</u>

<u>TOPPER 1</u>

- Had attended coaching classes and also did self study
- Clarified doubts through whatsapp groups
- Conscious of time and schedule
- Clear on concepts and consistent preparation helped. Gone fundementals and questions from past papers and practised them
- Guidance of senior students was useful
- Took private coaching

<u>TOPPER 2</u>

Had taken mock tests and checked the answers

Identified areas of mistakes

Studied again those chapters and understood fundamentals

Went through syllabus thoroughly

Attended some motivation classes

Worked out some extra sums for maths and physics

Revision is a must

Made a time table and studied

7a) <u>SCHOLARSHIP EXAMS</u>

NTSE, KVPY, INSPIRE-SEATS, INSPIRE-SHE, INSPIRE-MANAK, NMMS, TRUST, OLYMPIADS, HBCSE, NHFDC SCHOLARSHIPS, PRAGATI SCHOLARSHIP, SAKSHAM SCHOLARSHIP, SCIENCE OLYMPIAD FOUNDATION, AICTSD-ARYABHATTA NATIONAL MATHS COMPETITION, ARYABHATTA MATHS OLYMPIAD

<u>NTSE (NATIONAL TALENT SEARCH EXAM)</u>

CONDUCTED FOR 10TH STD STUDENTS FOR PROVIDING SCHOLARSHIPS EVERY YEAR TILL THEY CONTINUE THEIR STUDIES SAY UPTIL PhD.

<u>2 STAGES OF EXAM</u> - STAGE 1 & 2. STUDENTS WHO CLEARED STAGE 1 CAN APPEAR FOR STAGE 2. OBJECTIVE TYPE EXAM- NO NEGATIVE MARKS

<u>STAGE 1: OBJECTIVE TYPE EXAM :</u>

MAT (MENTAL ABILITY TEST)- 100 QUESTIONS- 90 MINUTES

SAT (SCHOLASTIC APTITUDE TEST)- 100 QUESTIONS- 90 MTS TEST IS CONDUCTED IN NOVEMBER / DECEMBER EVERY YEAR. APPLICATION HAS TO BE SUBMITTED IN AUGUST...AFTER THE NOTIFICATION AND FILLED APPLICATION IS TO BE SENT THROUGH THE SCHOOL TO : DIRECTORATE OF GOVERNMENT EXAMINATIONS.

EXAM FEE IS Rs 50/-. WEBSITE : www.dge.tn.gov.in

STAGE 2: CONDUCTED IN MAY NEXT YEAR

<u>**SCHOLASTIC ABILITY TEST**</u>- 100 QUESTIONS

<u>**MATHS**</u>- 20 QUESTIONS

CHAPTERS ARE : TIME AND WORK, TIME AND DISTANCE, GEOMETRY, MENSURATION, PERCENTAGES, INDICES, RATIO PROPORTION, STATISTICS, ARITHMETIC PROGRESSSION

<u>**SCIENCE**</u> (PHYSICS, CHEMISTRY , BOTONY AND ZOOLOGY)-40 QUESTIONS

<u>**SOCIAL SCEINCE**</u> (CIVICS, GEOGRAPHY, HISTORY, ECONOMICS)-40 QUESTIONS

<u>MENTAL ABILITY TEST (MAT)</u> - 100 QUESTIONS

TOPICS ARE:
DIRECTION SENSE, CODING/DECODING, BLOOD RELATIONSHIP, DEDUCTIONS, NUMBER SERIES, CLOCK, NUMBER ANALOGIES, LETTER SERIES , LETTER ANALOGIES , CALENDAR, VERBAL ANALOGIES, CUBE, VENN DIAGRAMS, MIRROR IMAGE, WATER IMAGE, ETC

Website :
https://ncert.nic.in ,   www.dge.tn.gov.in

<u>KVPY FELLOWSHIPS</u>
<u>Kishore Vaigyanik Protsahan Yojana (KVPY) - Scholarships</u>

The Kishore Vaigyanik Protsahan Yojana (KVPY) is an on-going National Program of Fellowship in Basic Sciences, initiated and funded by the Department of Science and Technology, Government of India, to attract exceptionally highly motivated students for pursuing basic science courses and research career in science.

Selection of the students is made from those studying in XI standard to 1st year of any undergraduate program in Basic Sciences namely B.Sc./B.S./B.Stat./B.Math./Int.M.Sc./M.S.in Mathematics, Physics, Chemistry and Biology having aptitude for scientific research.

BASIC SCIENCES	**Monthly Fellowship**	**Annual Contingency Grant**
SA/SX/SB - during 1st to 3rd years of B.Sc/BS/B Stat/B Math / Integrated M.Sc. /M.S.	Rs. 5000	Rs. 20000
SA/SX/SB - during M. Sc. / 4th to 5th years of Integrated M.Sc. /M.S./M.Math./M.Stat.	Rs. 7000	Rs. 28000

The fellowship for the students selected under the stream SA/SX/SB will be started after the XII Standard/ (+2) / I year UG, only if they pursue an undergraduate course in Basic Sciences, that are, B.Sc./B.S./B.Stat./B.Math./Int. M.Sc./M.S. in Chemistry, Physics, Mathematics, Statistics, Biochemistry, Microbiology, Cell Biology, Ecology, Molecular Biology, Botany, Zoology, Physiology, Biotechnology, Neurosciences, Bioinformatics, Marine Biology, Geology, Human Biology, Genetics, Biomedical Sciences, Applied Physics, Materials Science, Environmental Science or Geophysics.

Stream SA: Students who have enrolled in XI standard (Science subjects) during the academic year are eligible to appear for Aptitude test.

Stream SX: Students enrolled in XII Standard (Science subjects) during the academic year and aspiring to join undergraduate program in Basic Sciences (B.Sc./B.S./B.Stat./B.Math./Int. M.Sc./Int. M.S) during the academic year.

Stream SB: Students who have enrolled in the 1st year B.Sc./B.S./B.Stat./B.Math./Int. M.Sc./Int. M.S. during the academic year are eligible to appear for the aptitude test.

Aptitude Test: Candidates meeting the eligibility criteria for various streams, will be called for aptitude test conducted both in Hindi and English at different centers across the country in the month of May every year.
Website : www.kvpy.iisc.ernet.in

NMMS (National Merit cum Means Scholarship)

The National Means cum Merit Scholarship Examination (NMMS) is conducted every year by Science Branch of Directorate of Education, Delhi usually in the month of November for the students studying in class VIII of Govt./Aided schools. What is the scholarship amount of NMMS?

NMMS disburses a total of 100,000 scholarships every year at the rate of INR 12000 per annum, i.e. INR 1000 per month, to the selected students. Under National Means-Cum-Merit Scholarship, the scholarship amount is paid by State bank of India (SBI) on one go.

 how to ace competitive exams

NMMS Exam Syllabus for Scholastic Ability Test (SAT)

SAT under the NMMS will test the candidate's conceptual knowledge in three different sections, including Science, Social Studies, and Mathematics. All three subjects will have the syllabus taught in class 7th and 8th.

Marking Scheme: 1 Mark for each correct answer. No Negative Marking.

MENTAL ABILITY SYLLABUS

Direction sense, coding/devoding,blood relationship, number series and analogies, letter series and analogies, verbal analogies.

TAMIL NADU RURAL STUDENTS TALENT SEARCH EXAMINATION (TRUST)

Examination Date

The Examination is held in August last Sunday every year (only objective type question).

MENTAL ABILITY SYLLABUS

Direction sense, coding/devoding,blood relationship, number series and analogies, letter series and analogies, verbal analogies.

Eligibility

The Scholarship scheme for the Talented Rural Students shall be conducted for the students studying in the schools located in Rural Areas only.

The Students who are currently studying in IX std in recognized schools and Secured 50% of marks in VIII std. annual examination, parental annual Income does not exceed Rs. 1,00,000/- are eligible to apply for the above examination.

Submission of application

The blank application form can be had from the Chief Educational Officer. The Head of Institution will collect the form and issue the same to eligible willing Candidates. The filled in application with income certificate from Tashildar should be counter signed by the respective Headmasters / Headmistress and send to the Chief Educational officers.

Release of Results and Distribution of Certificates

The selected students under the scheme if detained or discontinued his / her studies will not eligible for Scholarship amount.

The results is given by Director of School Education, Chennai 6.

TTSE (Tamil Talent Search Exam)
This exam is conducted by TN Government for 11th std students. Student from any board and any medium can write this exam. This exam is conducted in Sept/Oct and announcement comes in June. 1500 students are selected based on this exam and are given Rs 1500/- per month for 11th and 12th std (2 years)

NHFDC (NATIONAL HANDICAPPED FINANCE DEVELOPMENT CORPORATION) SCHOLARSHIP

BENEFICIARIES : Differently abled students who want to pursue professional or technical courses

NUMBER OF SCHOLARSHIPS : 2500 per year. 30% is reserved for girls.

AMOUNT : Non refundable fees of govt or govt aided institutions. Maintenance charges of Rs 2500 per month and Rs 6000/ per annum for books for graduation courses.

Visual, Hearing and Orthopaedically handicapped differently-abled students, in addition will be provided with aids and appliances, only once during lifetime.

Condition : Annual family income should be less than Rs 3.0 lacs
Website : http://www.nhfdc.nic.in/scholarship.html

PRAGATI SCHOLARSHIP SCHEME FOR GIRL STUDENTS

Pragati is a MHRD Scheme being implemented by of AICTE aimed at providing assistance for Advancement of Girls pursuing Technical Education

For Girl students pursuing technical courses such as graduation or diploma in engineering

Total Number of Scholarship-4000 per Annum (2000 for Degree and 2000 for Diploma)

SAKSHAM SCHOLARSHIP SCHEME FOR SPECIALLY ABLED STUDENTS

Saksham is a MHRD scheme being implemented by of AICTE aimed at providing encouragement and support to specially abled children to pursue Technical Education.

Total Number of Scholarship-1000 per Annum (500 for Degree and 500 for Diploma)

Amount of scholarship for both the schemes: Tuition Fee of Rs. 30,000/- or at actual, whichever is less and Rs.2000/- per month for 10 months as incidentals charges each year. In case of Tuition fee waiver/reimbursement, Students are eligible to get an amount of Rs. 30,000/- for the purchase of Books/Equipment/Softwares/Laptop/Desktop/Vehicle /Fee paid towards competitive examination applications forms/exam/ specific equipments/ software's for visually impaired/ speech and hearing disabled.

Website : https://www.aicte-pragati-saksham-gov.in/

<u>**INSPIRE**</u>
<u>**Scheme for Early Attraction of Talent (SEATS)**</u>

(SEATS) aims to attract talented youth to study science by providing INSPIRE Award of Rs 5000 to one million young learners of the age group 10-15 years, ranging from Class VI to Class X standards, and also by arranging summer camps for about 50,000 science students of Class XI with global leaders in science to experience the joy of innovations on an annual basis through INSPIRE Internship.

<u>**Scholarship for Higher Education (SHE)**</u>

(SHE) aims to enhance rates of attachment of talented youth to undertake higher education in science intensive programmes, by providing scholarships and mentorship. The scheme offers 10,000 Scholarship every year at Rs 0.80 lakh per year for the talented youth in the age group 17-22 years, for undertaking Bachelor and Masters level education in natural sciences. The main feature of the scheme is the mentorship support provided to every scholar

https://online-inspire.gov.in/content/INSPIRE_Brochure.pdf

7b) AWARDS BASED ON COMPETITIONS

INSPIRE Awards-MANAK

The INSPIRE Awards - MANAK (Million Minds Augmenting National Aspirations and Knowledge), being executed by DST with National Innovation Foundation – India (NIF), an autonomous body of DST, aims to motivate students in the age group of 10-15 years and studying in classes 6 to 10. The objective of the scheme is to target one million original ideas/innovations rooted in science and societal applications to foster a culture of creativity and innovative thinking among school children. Under this scheme, schools can nominate 5 best original ideas/innovations of students through this website.

This scheme is being operationalised as per the following steps:

Organising internal idea competitions in schools and nominations of two to three best original ideas, in any Indian language, by the respective Principal/Headmaster online through E-MIAS (E-Management of INSPIRE Awards MANAK Scheme) portal. The schools should register themselves on E-MIAS portal. Shortlisting of top 1,00,000 (one lakh) ideas, with potential to address societal needs through Science & Technology by NIF.

Disbursement of INSPIRE Award of INR 10,000 into the bank accounts of short-listed students through Direct Benefit Transfer (DBT) scheme.

Organisation of District Level Exhibition and Project Competition (DLEPC) by District/State authorities and shortlisting of 10,000 best ideas/innovations for State Level Exhibition and Project Competitions (SLEPC).

Organisation of State Level Exhibition & Project Competition (SLEPC) for further shortlisting of top 1,000 ideas/innovations for the National Level Exhibition and Project Competition (NLEPC). At this stage, NIF will provide mentoring support to students for development of prototypes, in coordination with reputed academic and technology institutions of the country.

Selection of ideas/innovations will be based on novelty, social applicability, environment friendliness, user friendliness and comparative advantage over the existing similar technologies.

Showcasing 1,000 best ideas/innovations at the National Level Exhibition & Project Competition (NLEPC) and shortlisting of top 60 innovations for national awards and future direction.

Consideration of top 60 ideas/innovations by NIF for product/process development and their linkage with other schemes of NIF/DST and their display at the Annual Festival of Innovation & Entrepreneurship (FINE).

Website : https://www.inspireawards-dst.gov.in

OLYMPIADS HBCSE

Homi Bhaba Centre for Science Education, TIFR in association with Infosys Foundation and TIFR Endowment Fund conduct Olympiads for students from 6th-12th std. Based on that they award prizes.
Website : olympiads.hbcse.tifr.res.in

SCIENCE OLMPIAD FOUNDATION

Olympiad exams are conducted mostly through schools for students from 1st to 11th std. Prizes are given for winners.
Website : www.sofworld.org

ARYABHATTA NATIONAL MATHS COMPETITION

AICTSD-ARYABHATTA NATIONAL MATHS COMPETITION

They conduct many competition tests and give away awards.
Website: www.aictsd.com/anmc

ARYABHATTA MATHS OLYMPIAD

Prizes are given for winners from 1 - 8th std
Website : aryabhattamathsolympiad.com

8a) <u>EXAMS FOR JOB RECRUITMENT</u>

<u>Competitive exams for job recruitment are :</u>

TNPSC Group Exams(1-8),UPSC Exams (Civil Services, NDA,ESE,CDS,CAPF,IES)SSC Exams (CGL,CDSE,CHSL), GATE

<u>TNPSC GROUP 1 EXAM</u>

ANY DEGREE OR FINAL YEAR STUDENT;   AGE LIMIT 37
STAGE 1 : PRELIMINARY EXAM / 200 Qns / 300 MARKS
             GENERAL STUDIES 175 Qns & MAT 25 Qns
STAGE 2 : MAINS – 3 PAPERS EACH IN GENERAL STUDIES OF
             250 MARKS EACH
STAGE 3 : INTERVIEW – 100 MARKS

PRELIMINARY EXAM – SYLLABUS

1. General Science 2. Current Events / Current Affairs 3. Geography of India 4. History and Culture of India 5. Indian Polity 6. Indian Economy 7. Indian-National Movement 8. History, Culture, Heritage, & Socio-Political Movements in TN 9. Development Administration in Tamil Nadu 10. Aptitude and Mental Ability

POSTS : Deputy Collector, DSP, District Registrar, District Employment Officer, Divisional Officer in Fire & Rescue Services, Asst Commissioner

TNPSC GROUP 1A ; POSTS : Assistant Conservator of Forests
TNPSC GROUP 1B ; POSTS : Assistant Commissioner - HR & CE
TNPSC GROUP 1C ; POSTS : District Educational Officer
ELIGIBILITY : Graduation

TNPSC GROUP 2 EXAM

Eligibility : Any Degree;   Age : 18-30
Language : Tamil or English
With interview : About 35% posts
Without interview : 65% posts
Exam : Preliminary and Main Exam
Preliminiary Exam : Objective Type Exam / 200 questions/ 300 marks
General Studies - 175 questions; Mental Ability - 25 questions
Main Exam : Written Exam
Part A : Translation - 100 marks
Part B : Precis Writing, Hints Development, Essay Writing on Thirukural, letter writing, Comprehension - 200 marks

TNPSC GROUP 2 with Interview

POSTS : Assistant Sales Tax officer, Assistant Employment Officer, Assitant Registrar, Jobs in departments viz Law/ Finance/ Legislative Assembly/ Prison/ Coopcrative Society, Handloom, Guest House, Tribal Welfare, Milk Cooperative Society, Audit, Highways etc

TNPSC GROUP 2A (without interview)

POSTS : Jobs in departments viz Treasury, Accounts, Steno Typist, Public Works, Ministry, Finance etc
ELIGIBILITY ; Graduation

TNPSC GROUP 3
POSTS : Fire Service Officer

TNPSC GROUP 3A
POSTS : Junior Inspectors in Cooperative Societies, Assistant Supervisors
ELIGIBILITY ; Graduation

TNPSC GROUP 4 EXAM
POSTS: Typist, VAO, Junior Assistant, Bill Collector, Field Surveyor etc
Eligibility : 10th Std, Age : 18-35 years
Exam: 200 objective type questions and 300 marks and each question carry 1.5 marks. (General Studies - 75; Aptitude -25; General Tamil/English - 100)
Language : Tamil or English. Websites : www.tnpscexams.net, www.tnpscexams.in

TNPSC GROUP 5A EXAM
Post : Assistant in the Departments of Secretariat
ELIGIBILITY ; GRADUATION

TNPSC GROUP 6 EXAM : Post : Trainer in Forest Department

TNPSC GROUP 7A : Post : Officer in Administration Department - Grade 1

TNPSC GROUP 7B : Post : Officer in Administration Department - Grade 3

TNPSC GROUP 8 : Post : Officer in Administration Department - Grade 4

TNPSC Combined Engineering Services

Tamil Nadu Public Service Commission conducts the Engineering Services Exam ESE for the recruitment of Group B (Class-II) engineers in the state government departments and ministries. Candidates bearing engineering degrees in the relevant field from a recognized university or institute and falling under the age criteria are eligible to apply for this decent-paying govt job.
ELIGIBILITY ; BE or B Tech

TNPSC Assistant Engineer

Candidates aspiring for the Tamil Nadu Assistant Engineer (ASE) posts must go through the eligibility criteria set by the TNPSC. Generally, candidates aged less than 30 years of age having completed their graduation in the relevant engineering field are eligible to apply for the Assistant Engineer posts.
ELIGIBILITY ; BE or B Tech

TNPSC District Education Officer

To become a District Education Officer (DEO) in Tamil Nadu, candidates must appear for the TNPSC DEO Exam 2022. The educational requirement for the same is Master's Degree in any relevant subject with B.Ed course from a government recognized university or institute.

ELIGIBILITY : Master's degree, a B.T., or a B.Ed. Degree

UPSC (UNION PUBLIC SERVICE COMMISSION)
UPSC /CIVIL SERVICES EXAM/IAS EXAM

Following are the services which one gets on qualifying the Civil Service Examination.

All India Services

Indian Administrative Service (IAS), Indian Police Service (IPS)

Central Services (Group A)

Indian Foreign Service (IFS), Indian Audit and Accounts Service (IA&AS), Indian Civil Accounts Service (ICAS), Indian Corporate Law Service (ICLS), Indian Defence Accounts Service (IDAS), Indian Defence Estates Service (IDES), Indian Information Service (IIS), Indian Postal Service (IPoS), Indian P&T Accounts and Finance Service (IP&TAFS), Indian Railway Management Service (IRMS), Indian Railway Protection Force Service (IRPFS), Indian Revenue Service (IRS-IT), Indian Revenue Service (IRS-C&CE),Indian Trade Service (ITrS)

Group B Services

Armed Forces Headquarters Civil Services (AFHCS), Delhi, Andaman and Nicobar Islands Civil Service (DANICS), Delhi, Andaman and Nicobar Islands Police Service (DANIPS), Pondicherry Civil Service (PCS), Pondicherry Police Service (PPS)

TOTAL APPLICATIONS : 9 LACS; AFTER PRELIMINARY EXAM 20000 ARE SELECTED TO WRITE MAIN EXAM. ABOUT 2000 ARE SELECTED FOR INTERVIEW BASED ON PERFORMANCE ON MAINS; FINAL SELECTION IS ABOUT 1000 INCLUDING THE WAITING LIST

<u>PRELIMINARY</u> – 2 PAPERS

PAPER-1 : GENERAL AFFAIRS, HISTORY, GEOGRAPHY, CIVICS, ECONOMICS, ENVIRONMENT, GEN SCIENCE (200 marks)/2 hours

PAPER-2 : COMPREHENSION, ENGLISH, MENTAL ABILITY, DATA INTREPRETATION, DATA SUFFICIENCY, BASIC MATHS, REASONING, (200marks) / 2hours - THIS IS A QUALIFYING PAPER WITH MINIMUM MARKS OF 33%

LANGUAGE – HINDI AND ENGLISH

<u>MAIN EXAM</u>

PAPER A & B – QUALIFYING PAPER ON ENGLISH AND ONE INDIAN LANGUAGE – 300 MARKS EACH. MARKS OBTAINED IS NOT COUNTED FOR FINAL MERIT LIST

<u>PAPER COUNTED FOR MERIT LIST –</u>

TOTAL MARKS – 1750

PAPER 1- ESSAY;   **PAPER 2 TO 5**   GENERAL STUDIES OF 250 MARKS EACH **PAPER 6 & 7** – OPTIONAL SUBJECTS – 250 MARKS EACH 3 HOURS EACH   ENGLISH OR HINDI EXCEPT LANGUAGE. PERSONALITY TEST (INTERVIEW) - MARKS – 275   TOTAL MARKS - 2025
Website : www.upsc.gov.in

<u>UPSC - NDA (NATIONAL DEFENCE ACADEMY)</u>

ELIGIBILITY - 12TH STD
POST IN AIRFORCE AND NAVY
WRITTEN TEST AND SSB INTERVIEW

 how to ace competitive exams

UPSC - ESE (ENGINEERING SERVICES)

ELIGIBILITY - BE / BTECH
-CIVIL, MECH, ELECTRICAL, TELE COMMUNICATION & OTHER BRANCHES
-JOBS IN RAILWAYS, NAVAL ARMAMENT, DEFENCE, BORDER ROADS, POWER ETC
- PRELIMINARY EXAM, MAIN EXAM AND INTERVIEW

UPSC-CDS (COMBINED DEFENCE SERVICES)

FOR OFFICER CATEGORY POSTS IN ARMY, AIRFORCE & MILITARY
INDIAN MILITARY ACADEMY, INDIAN NAVAL ACADEMY, INDIAN AIRFORCE ACADEMY, OFFICERS TRAINING ACADEMY (BOTH MALE & FEMALE)
-TESTS ARE MCQs IN GK, ENGLISH, MATHS - 100 MARKS EACH - 120 QUESTIONS

UPSC - CAPF (CENTRAL ARMED POLICE FORCES)

ASSISTANT COMMANDANTS IN BSF, CISF, CRPF,SSB & ITBP
PAPER 1- GK, MENTAL ABILITY, SOCIAL SCIENCE AND SCIENCE
PAPER 2 - GK, ESSAY, COMPREHENSION

UPSC - IES (INDIAN ECONOMIC SERVICES) / ISS(INDIAN STATISTICAL SERVICES)

- ELIGIBILITY - DEGREE IN ECONOMICS OR STATISTICS
- WRITTEN TEST FOR 1000 MARKS
IES - ENGLISH, GK, ECONOMICS - 4 PAPERS
ISS - ENGLISH, GK, STATISTICS - 4 PAPERS

COMBINED MEDICAL SERVICE EXAMINATION (CMS)

The Combined Medical Services Examination or the CMS Examination is conducted by the Union Public Service Commission for recruitment as Medical Officer in various organisations such as the Indian Ordnance Factories, Indian Railways, Municipal Corporation of Delhi, New Delhi Municipal Council functioning under the Government of India

Read more at : www.careerindia.com/upsc/cms-exam-e19.html

COMBINED GEO-SCIENTIST AND GEOLOGIST EXAM (CGGE) Exam

Union Public Service Commission (UPSC) conducts a Combined Geo-Scientist and Geologist Examination (CGGE) for recruitment and selection to the post of Geologist, Geophysicist and Chemist Group 'A' in GSI and Junior Hydro-geologist (Scientist 'B'), Group 'A' for Central Ground Water Board.

Read more at: https://www.careerindia.com/upsc/cgge-exam-e22.html

CBI (CENTRAL BUREAU OF INVESTIGATION)

Step 1 – Complete your graduation from a recognized university. Step 2 – For becoming CBI Sub Inspector, apply for the SSC-CGL exam and clear it. Step 3 – For becoming a Direct Grade-A officer in CBI, Apply for UPSC civil services exam and crack it and become an IPS officer.

They also recruit IT cell specialists and other Group C posts through SSC exam.

Age Limit for SSC - CGL candidates is 20-25

Age Limit for UPSC Candidates 21-32

There are physical standards required to join CBI.

Websites :www.ssc.nic.in and www.upsc.gov.in

<u>**SSC (STAFF SELECTION COMMISSION)**
CGL EXAM (COMBINED GRADUATE LEVEL)</u>

Exam is conducted for about 8-10k vacancies every year in Central Govt Departments & Ministries viz IT, GST, Customs etc departments and all ministries to fill Assistants and Inspectors. Eligibility : Any Degree Languages : English & Hindi, Age Limit : Upto 27 for some posts and Upto 30 for some posts. Exam centres in TN : Chennai, Coimbatore, Madurai, Trichy, Tirunelveli, Salem & Vellore;   4 Tier Exam

Tier 1 - 60 minutes- Computer Based test (CBT) with 4 sections viz reasoning, GK, Quantitative, English;   100 Questions and 200 Marks

Candidates clearing Tier 1 , can write Tier 2 & 3

Tier 2 - 4 Paper - Computer Based Test - 2 Hours

Tier 3 - Pen & Paper (Descriptive) - 60 minutes

Tier 4 - Pen & Paper (Descriptive) - 45 minutes

Website : www.ssc.nic.in

<u>**SSC - CDSE**</u>

The Combined   Defence   Services Examination (abbreviated as CDS Exam) is conducted by the Union Public Service Commission for recruitment of Commissioned Officers in the Indian Military Academy, Officers Training Academy, Indian Naval Academy and Indian Air Force Academy.

Graduate students are applicable for CDS Entry

Website : http://upsconline.nic.in

Course and Training shall be given in one of the following academy

1. Indian Military Academy, Dehradun 2. Indian Naval Academy, Ezhimala

3. Air Force Academy, Hyderabad—(Pre-Flying) 4. Officers' Training Academy, Chennai (Madras) 5. Officers Training Academy, Chennai (Madras)(Women)

SSC CHSL (COMBINED HIGHER SECONDARY LEVEL EXAM)

SSC CHSL is a combined competition exam conducted to select Higher Secondary qualified students into various departments and offices of the government.

SSC GD CONSTABLE EXAM

The minimum educational qualification to apply for the post of SSC GD exam is 10th pass. The recruitment process for SSC GD will consist of Computer Based Examination (CBE), Physical Efficiency Test (PET), Physical Standard Test (PST), and Detailed Medical Examination (DME).
Website : www.ssc.nic.in

SSC JE EXAM

SSC JE is an exam conducted by Staff Selection Commission (SSC). This exam is meant for the recruitment of Junior Engineers (JEs) in various branches of Engineering including Civil, Electrical, Mechanical and Quantity Surveying & Contracts.
Website : www.ssc.nic.in

SSC MTS EXAM

Staff Selection Commission Multi Tasking Staff Exam. SSC MTS exam is a national level exam conducted by the Staff Selection Commission (SSC) for selecting candidates in General Central Service Group-C non-gazetted, non-ministerial posts in various ministries, departments and offices of the Govt of India. Havaldar , Peon, Daftary, Jamadar, Junior Gestetner Operator, Chowkidar, Safaiwala, Mali etc.
Website : www.ssc.nic.in

GATE EXAM (GRADUATE APTITUDE TEST IN ENGINEERING)

Purpose : Entry into Master's Program in Engineering (ME/MTech)

Job in public sector companies viz BHEL, CIL, GAIL, IOCL, NTPC, ONGC, SAIL, BPCL, BEL, CCI, EIL, HAL, HPCL, MTNL, NACL, NBCL, NMDC, NLC, OIL, Power Finance Corporation Ltd, Power Grid Corporation of India Ltd, Rashtriya Ispat Nigam Ltd, Rural Electrification Corpn Ltd, Shipping Corporation of I Ltd, MECON, Engineering Projects I Ltd, Bharat Pumps & Compressors Ltd, FCI Aravali Gypsum & Minerals I Ltd, Artificial Limbs Mfg Corpn of India, etc

GATE is a Computer Based Test (CBT) exam in 27 subjects for 3 hours

General Aptitude + Candidate's Selected Subject

Total Marks = 100. Validity is 3 years from date of announcement of results

BANK EXAMS

Popular Bank Exams are SBI(State Bank of India) Exams, IBPS (Institute of Banking Personnel Selection) Exams, RBI (Reserve Bank of India) Exams, NABARD (National Bank for Agricultural and Rural Development) IPPB -(The India Post Payments Bank) Exams.

Bank Exams comprises of Preliminary, Mains, Group Discussion and Personal Interview. Following are the three types of Bank Exams : Clerical, Officers, RRB-Regional Rural Banks and Specialist Officers Exams.

9a) ENTRANCE EXAMS FOR HIGHER STUDIES

ENGINEERING
Joint Entrance Examination (JEE) Main
Purpose - For Admission in B. E./B. Tech., B. Arch.,
B.Planning in NITs, IIITs etc
Eligibility - Class 12 pass (PCM)
Application mode – Online

JEE Advanced
Purpose- Admission in UG programme in IITs
Eligibility - Class 12 Pass (PCM)
Application mode –Online

BITSAT
Purpose - Admission in Integrated First Degree
programme in BITS Pilani, Goa & Hyderabad
campuses.
Eligibility - Class 12 pass (PCM)
Application mode - Online

MEDICAL
National Eligibility Cum Entrance Test (NEET)
Purpose-Admission to MBBS/BDS/AYUSH courses
Eligibility-Class 12 (PCB)
Application mode - Online

Humanity & Social Sciences

Humanities and Social Sciences Entrance Examination (HSEE)

Purpose-Admission in integrated Master of Arts (M.A.) program in IIT Madras
Eligibility- Class 12
Application mode - Online
Source: http://hsee.iitm.ac.in/

TISS Bachelors Admission Test (TISS-BAT)

Purpose-Admission in B.A. Social Sciences program in any of three Campuses i.e. Tuljapur, Guwahati and Hyderabad
Eligibility- Class 12,
Application mode -Online
Source: http://tiss.edu/admissions

Agriculture & Hotel Management:

Indian Council of Agricultural Research ICAR AIEEA-UG

Purpose-Admission in Bachelor Degree Program, at Agricultural Universities
Eligibility-Class 12 for UG

Mathematics

Indian Statistical Institute Admission

Purpose-Admission in B Stat (Hons), B Math (Hons), M Stat, M Math, MS (QE), MS (LIS), M Tech (CS), M Tech (QROR) and Research Fellowships.
Eligibility-Class 12 (Maths, English)
Application mode -Online, By Post
Source: www.isical.ac.in/index.php

Chennai Mathematical Institute (CMI)

BSc Hons (maths and computer science)

BSc Hons (maths and physics) 3 years course

Admission is through an entrance exam conducted in May month for students who have appeared or completed 12th

Website : www.cmi.ac.in

Fashion & Design

National Institute of Fashion Technology (NIFT)

Purpose-For Admission in Design, Management and Technology for the international fashion business

Eligibility- Class 12,

Application mode -Online, By Post

Source: www.nift.ac.in/

National Institute of Design

Purpose-Admission to 4 year GDPD & 2.5 Year PGDPD

Eligibility- Class 12

Application mode -By Post

Source: www.admissions.nid.edu/

All India Entrance Examination for Design (AIEED)

Purpose-Admission in 4 years UG level program in Design

Eligibility-Class 11, 12   Application mode - Online

Source: **www.aieed.com/**

UCEED Written Exam

B Design program - Product Design, IDC IIT Bombay Communication Design, Interaction Design, Mobility Design and Animation Design www.uceed.in/

Footwear Design and Development Institute (FDDI All India Selection Test) Computer Based Entrance Test Footwear Design **www.fddiindia.com/**

Pure Science
Kishore Vaigyanik Protsahan Yojana (KVPY)

Purpose-Fellowship and admission to IISc Banglore in 4 year BS Degree
Eligibility- Class 11, 12,
Application mode - Online, in Person, By Post
Source: http://kvpy.iisc.ernet.in/main/index.htm

Indian Institutes of Science Education and Research

Purpose-Admissions to 5 year BS-MS Degree Programme
Eligibility- Class 12
Application mode - Online
Source: https://www.iiseradmission.in/

National Entrance Screening Test (NEST)

Purpose-Admission in 5 year integrated M.Sc. programme in Biological, Chemical, Mathematical and Physical sciences in NISER or UM-DAE CBS.
Eligibility-Class 12 (PCMB)
Application mode - Online, By Post
Source: www.nestexam.in/

Integrated MSc Course

NEST Exam for The National
EDUCATION: RIE-CEE.
Written Exam for 5 year integrated M Sc. Course in
Biology, Chemistry, Mathematics and
Physics www.niser.ac.in/

Other Integrated MSc Courses

Individual colleges conduct entrance exams and admit
based on board marks + entrance exam marks
- Theoretical Computer Science
- Software Systems
- Data Science

Integrated MBA Course

Offered by IIM Indore. It is a five year course.
Admission is through an entrance exam conducted by
IIM Indore.
Website : www.iimidr.ac.in

HOTEL MANAGEMENT

Hotel Management courses admission is done through
a common entrance exam. Websites which give
details are : www.nta.ac.in/hotel management and
www.nchm.nic.in

EDUCATION

Regional Institute of Education RIE CEE Written
Exam B.Sc. B.Ed. / BA B.Ed 4 Year / M Sc B
Ed www.rieajmer.raj.nic.in/

CENTRAL UNIVERSITIES
CUET
Central Universities Common Entrance Test (CUET)
Written Exam
UG / PG and Research Programs of Central
Universities admit students through CUET.
Integrated M Sc courses are also offered.

RAILWAYS/TRANSPORT COURSES
These courses are conducted at their premises in
Vadodara
BSc (Transport) and BBM (Transport) courses are
offered

NATIONAL DEFENCE ACADEMY
BSc (Computer Science), BA, BCA, B Tech courses
are offered by this institute
Website give information : www.upsconline.nic.in

NAVAL ACADEMY , KERALA
BTech course is offered
Website : www.joinindiannavy.gov.in

ENTRANCE EXAMS FOR POST GRADUATE COURSES
1. TANCET - ME, MTech, MBA, MCA, M Arch, M Plan
2. NEET PG - PG MEDICAL COURSES
3. GATE - ME, MTech
4. CAT - MBA   5. MAT - MBA   6. CLAT PG - Post
graduate Law Courses

9b) DETAILS OF SOME ENTRANCE TESTS
JEE MAIN

About JEE (Main) -   The Joint Entrance Examination, JEE (Main) comprises two papers. Paper 1 is conducted for admission to Undergraduate Engineering Programs (B.E/B.Tech.) at NITs, IIITs, other Centrally Funded Technical Institutions (CFTIs), Institutions/Universities funded/recognized by participating State Governments. JEE (Main) is also an eligibility test for JEE (Advanced), which is conducted for admission to IITs.

Paper 2 is conducted for admission to B. Arch and B. Planning courses in the Country. The JEE (Main) is be conducted in 02 (two) sessions for admissions. The candidates will thus benefit in the following ways: This will give two opportunities to the candidates to improve their scores in the examination if they are not able to give their best in one attempt.

A candidate need not appear in both Sessions. However, if a candidate appears in more than one Session then his/her best of the JEE (Main) NTA Scores will be considered for preparation of Merit List/ Ranking. The total number of questions to be attempted are

IMPORTANT INFORMATION AT A GLANCE

1. Important Dates :
EVENTS DATES (a) Session-1 (April) : JEE (Main) : Online Submission of Application Form is in March . First week of April - Downloading of Admit Cards from NTA website. Second week of April - Dates of Examination
(b) Session-2 (May) : JEE (Main) : Online Submission of Application April end or May first week and Exam is conducted end of May

(c) Duration of Examination for each Session: JEE (Main) - : Paper 1 (B.E./B.Tech) or Paper 2A (B.Arch) or Paper 2B (B.Planning) - 3 Hours B.Arch & B.Planning (both) 3 Hours 30 Minutes (Mode of Examination JEE (Main) will be conducted in the following modes: a) Paper 1 (B.E. /B. Tech.) in "Computer Based Test (CBT)" mode only.

d) Paper 2A (B. Arch): Mathematics (Part-I) and Aptitude Test (Part-II) in "Computer Based Test (CBT)" mode only and Drawing Test (Part-III) in pen and paper (offline) mode, to be attempted on drawing sheet of A4 size.

e) Paper 2B (B. Planning): Mathematics (Part-I), Aptitude Test (Part-II), and Planning Based Questions (Part-III) in Computer Based Test (CBT) mode only.

2. Choice of Medium of Question Papers Medium of the Question Papers: English, Hindi, Assamese, Bengali, Gujarati, Kannada, Malayalam, Marathi, Odia, Punjabi, Tamil, Telugu, and Urdu. The option of language for Question Paper should be exercised while filling up the Application Form online and it cannot be changed at a later stage. Language / Examination Centres 1. English in All Examination Centres 2. English and Hindi in All Examination Centres in India 3. English and Tamil in All Examination Centres in Tamilnadu

3. Marking Scheme for MCQs - Correct Answer or the Most Appropriate Answer Four marks (+4). Incorrect Answer Minus one mark (-1), Unanswered / Marked for Review No mark (0)

4. Marking Scheme for questions for which the answer is a Numerical value Correct Answer Four marks (+4), Incorrect Answer Minus one mark (-1), Unanswered / Marked for Review No mark (0)

5. Year of Appearance in Qualifying Examination - Only those candidates who have passed the Class 12/equivalent examination in the past 2 years or those who are appearing in Class 12/equivalent examination in the current year, are eligible to appear in JEE (Main).

<u>**NEST EXAM (NATIONAL ENTRANCE SCREENING TEST)**</u>

For 5 year Integrated MSc Programs in Biology, Chemistry, Maths, Physics

Total - 250 seats

Institutes - NISER (National Institute of Science Education & Research), Bhuvaneswar; Dept of Atomic Energy Centre for Excellence in basic Science (UM-DAE CEBS), University of Mumbai

Eligibility : 12th Pass with 60% marks

<u>MEDICINE</u>
<u>NEET UG</u>
<u>Pattern of the Test</u>

The Test pattern of NEET (UG) - 2022 comprises four Subjects. Each subject will consist of two sections. Section A will consist of 35 Questions and Section B will have 15 Questions for each subject. Out of these 15 Questions, candidates can choose to attempt any 10 Questions. So, the total number of questions and utilization of time will remain the same. The pattern for the NEET (UG) Examination for admission is as follows:

Important Points to Note: (a) For Section A (MCQs): To answer a question, the candidates need to choose one option corresponding to the correct answer or the most appropriate answer. (i) Correct answer or the most appropriate answer: Four marks (+4) (ii) Any incorrect option marked will be given minus one mark (-1). (iii) Unanswered/Marked for Review will be given no mark (0). (iv) If more than one option is found to be correct then Four marks (+4) will be awarded to only those who have marked any of the correct options. (v) If all options are found to be correct then Four marks (+4) will be awarded to all those who have attempted the question.

   how to ace competitive exams

For Section B (MCQs): Candidates need to attempt any 10 Questions out of 15 Questions given. In the event of a candidate has attempted more than 10 questions, only the first 10 attempted questions will be considered for evaluation. There will also be negative marking for Section B.   vii. Candidates are advised to do the calculations with the constants given (if any) in the questions.

MCQ (Multiple Choice Questions)

1. PHYSICS: SECTION A- (35Qs)
        & 140 marks / SECTION B- (15Qs)& 40 marks
2. CHEMISTRY: SECTION A- (35Qs)
        & 140 marks/SECTION B -(15Qs) & 40 marks
3. BOTANY: SECTION A- (35Qs)
        & 140 marks / SECTION B - (15Qs and 40 marks
4. ZOOLOGY: SECTION A (35Qs)
        & 140 marks /SECTION B - 15 Qs) and 40 marks

TOTAL MARKS 720

Mode of Examination

NEET (UG) is a Pen & Paper-based Test, to be answered on the specially designed machine gradable OMR sheet using Ball Point Pen provided at the Centre.

Duration of Test

The duration of the test would be three (03) hours and 20 minutes. Candidates can opt for a Question Paper in any one of the 13 languages including English and Tamil. In case of any ambiguity in the translation of a question in the test, its English version shall be treated as final and the decision of NTA shall be final in this regard.

Candidates qualifying for NEET (UG) would be eligible for All India Quota and other quotas under the State Governments/Institutes.

<u>Eligibility to appear in NEET (UG)</u> – He/she has completed 17 years of age at the time of admission or will complete that age on or before 31 December of the year of his/her admission to the first year of the Undergraduate Medical Course.

Admissions to all seats of Undergraduate Medical / Dental Courses will be done through NEET (UG). The following are the seats available under different quotas: • All India Quota Seats • State Government Quota Seats • Central Institutions/Universities/Deemed Universities • State/Management/NRI Quota Seats in Private Medical / Dental Colleges or any Private University • Central Pool Quota Seats • All seats including NRI Quota as well as Management Quota, are in private unaided/aided minority / non-minority medical colleges. • AIIMS Institutes across India/JIPMER. •

The Counselling for successful candidates for Seats under 15% All India Quota separately. The counselling for admission to the seats under the control of State Governments/ UT Administrations / State Universities/ Institutions shall be conducted by the designated authorities of the State Governments as per the notifications issued separately by the authorities concerned.

An All India Merit List of the qualified candidates shall be prepared based on All India Rank in the Merit List of the NEET (UG) and candidates shall be admitted to Undergraduate Medical Courses from the said list only, with existing reservation policy.

<u>CLAT</u>

1. There will be no upper age limit for UG Programme in CLAT
2. As regards minimum percentage of marks in the qualifying examination (i.e., 10+2 or an equivalent examination), the candidates must have secured: Forty five percent (45%) marks or its equivalent grade in case of candidates belonging to General / OBC / PWD / NRI / PIO / OCI categories. Forty Percent (40%) marks or equivalent in case of candidates belonging to SC/ST categories.
3. Candidates who are appearing in the qualifying examination in March/April of the current year are also eligible to appear in CLAT

<u>Introduction and Overview</u>

The UG-CLAT would focus on evaluating the comprehension and reasoning skills and abilities of candidates. Overall, it is designed to be a test of aptitude and skills that are necessary for a legal education rather than prior knowledge, though prior knowledge occasionally may be useful to respond to questions in the Current Affairs section.

The UG-CLAT shall be a 2-hour test, with 150 multiple-choice questions carrying 1 mark each. There shall be negative marking of 0.25 marks for every wrong answer. These questions would be divided across the following 5 subjects:

English Language; Current Affairs, including General Knowledge; Legal Reasoning; Logical Reasoning; Quantitative Techniques

Maximum Marks - 150; Duration of CLAT Exam - 02:00 Hours

Multiple-Choice Questions; 150 questions of one mark each

Negative Marking - 0.25 Mark for each wrong answer

The application submission for CLAT is through online.

ICAR

The Indian Council of Agricultural Research (ICAR) is the apex body for managing research and education in agriculture in the entire country under the aegis of DARE, Ministry of Agriculture and Farmers Welfare.

The ICAR-AU System of India has 74 Agricultural Universities comprising 63 State Agricultural, Veterinary, Horticultural and Fisheries Universities (SAUs), 4 ICAR-DUs, viz. IARI, IVRI, NDRI and CIFE, 3 Central Agricultural Universities (CAU, Imphal, Dr. RPCAU, Pusa and RLB CAU, Jhansi), 4 Central Universities (CUs) having Faculty of Agriculture (BHU, AMU, Viswa Bharati and Nagaland University).

The National Agricultural Research and Education and Extension System (NAREES) of India is admitting more than 28,000 students at UG level and over 17,500 students at the PG and Doctoral level annually, in different disciplines of Agriculture and Allied Sciences.

ICAR has entrusted to the National Testing Agency(NTA), the task of conducting its Entrance and Fellowship Examinations mentioned below.

- ICAR AIEEA (UG) - is All India Entrance Examination for (a) admission to 15% seats in *Bachelor Degree Programme* in Agriculture and Allied Sciences (Other than veterinary sciences) at Agricultural Universities (100% seats at NDRI Karnal, RLBCAU Jhansi & DR. RPCAU PUSA) and (b) award of National Talent Scholarship in Agriculture & Allied Science subjects (other than Veterinary Science).

- Registration starts in June and Exam is in August

ICAR AIEEA Eligibility Criteria

Following are the complete list of <u>eligibility criteria</u> candidates will have to full fill to be eligible for admission:

For UG Courses:

- Qualification: Candidates should have passed 10+2 intermediate or its equivalent examination from any recognized board.

- Marks: Applying candidates should have score minimum of 50% Marks

- Age Limit: Candidates should be at least 16 years as on 31st August of that year

- Subject: Candidates should have PCB/PCMB/ PCM/Inter-Agriculture as mandatory subject to be eligible for examination.

ICAR AIEEA Exam Pattern

Following are the complete <u>exam pattern</u> for ICAR AIEEA UG Examination:

Mode of Examination: The exam will be conducted through LAN Based CBT (Computer Based Test).

Questions Type: There will be Multiple Choice Questions(MCQ) in the question paper.

Total Questions: There will be total of 150 questions in Question paper.

Total Marks: Question paper will be for maximum 600 marks.

Duration: Exam Duration will be of 2 hour and 30 Minutes.

Medium: Question paper will be in English & Hindi language.

Marking scheme: Each right answer will consist of 4 marks and 1 marks will be deducted on every incorrect answer.

NATA

Examination is conducted in two sessions. The two tests shall be held on June /July and August respectively.

Number of Questions - 125 ; Marks - 200

The questions will carry 1 mark, 2 marks or 3 marks and 125 questions have to be answered in 180 minutes.

The medium of Aptitude test will be essentially English language. Some questions may be in regional languages also. The aptitude of the candidate will be assessed using some or all of the following techniques:

Questions could be asked in various topics that assess candidates on basic concepts in mathematics, physics and geometry, language and interpretation, elements and principles of design, aesthetic sensitivity, colour theory, lateral thinking and logical reasoning, visual perception and cognition, graphics and imagery, building anatomy and architectural vocabulary, basic techniques of building construction and knowledge of material, general knowledge and current affairs, etc. and are may not be limited to those outlined.

Eligibility Criteria for Candidates - Candidates who have completed or appearing in the current year their 10 + 2 examination with Physics, Chemistry and Mathematics or 10+ 3 Diploma with Mathematics as subject of study can appear for NATA . Candidates may note that NATA is the qualifier for admission to B.Arch. program offered by Universities/ Institutions in the country, subject to the fulfillment of eligibility criteria as prescribed by the Council.

<u>JAM (JOINT ADMISSION TEST)</u>

Test for admission to MSc courses in 20 IITs
Online CBT Exam   Eligibility : Degree
7 Test paper : Biotechnology, Maths, Physics, Chemistry,
Mathematical Science, Economics

9c) <u>Competitive Exams to Study Abroad</u>

When it comes to studying abroad, it is imperative to know that different universities and countries have their own set of examinations. This can further be categorised into subject-based tests. However, there are some common <u>exams to study abroad</u> which have been given a run down below.

<u>International English Language Testing System (IELTS)</u>

IELTS tests your basic skills in the English language. You can get admission in countries like Canada, the US, UK, Australia, etc.

<u>Test of English as Foreign Language (TOEFL)</u>

TOEFL a standardized language proficiency test. The score of this test is accepted by various universities to offer admissions.

<u>Law School Admission Test (LSAT)</u>

This is a competitive exam conducted after 12th to help students secure admission in the <u>top law school of the world</u>.

<u>Medical College Admission Test (MCAT)</u>

The non-native students willing to secure admission in the <u>Medical field in Canada</u> and the US have to go through this MCAT examination after 12th.

<u>GRE (Graduate Record Examination)</u>

GRE is conducted to help students pursue a master's or doctoral program in the US, Canada, Australia etc. This exam is given after graduation

<u>Graduate Management Admission Test (GMAT)</u>

To pursue <u>MBA abroad</u>, giving the GMAT exam is a must after the graduation.

10a) <u>STATE & CENTRAL UNIVERSITIES IN TN</u>

<u>Universities in Tamilnadu</u>

1. Tamil University (website : www.tamiluniversity.ac.in)
2. Madras University (website : www.unom.ac.in)
3. Anna University (website : www.annauniv.edu)
4. Tiruvalluvar University (website : www.tvu.edu.in)
5. Annamalai University (website : www.annamalaiuniversity.ac.in)
6. Bharathidasan University (website : www.bdu.ac.in)
7. Bharathiar University (website : www.b-u.ac.in)
8. Periyar University (website : www.periyaruniversity.ac.in)

9. Madurai Kamaraj University (website :
www.mkuniversity.ac.in)
10. Manomaniam University (website :
www.msuniv.ac.in)
11. Annai Therasa University (website :
www.mothertherasawomenuniv.ac.in)
12. Tamilnadu Agricultural University (website :
www.tn.ac.in)
13. Dr J Jayalalitha Fisheries University (website :
www.tnjfu.ac.in)
14. Ambedkar Law University (website :
www.tndalu.ac.in)
15. MGR Medical University (website:
www.tnmgrmu.ac.in)
16. J Jayalalitha Music University (website :
www.tnjjmfau.in)
17. Teachers Education University (website :
www.tnteu.ac.in)
18. Sports University (website : www.tnpesu.org)
19. TN Open University (website : www.tnou.ac.in)

<u>CENTRAL UNIVERSITIES AND INSTITUTIONS IN TN (WEBSITES)</u>

1. Central Electrochemical Laboratory,Karaikudi
(www.cecri.res.in)
2. Central University of TN, Tiruvarur
(www.cutn.ac.in)
3. Indian Institute of Technology, Chennai
(www.iitm.ac.in)
4. National Institute of Technology, Trichy
(www.nitt.edu)

5. National Institute of Fashion Technology, Chennai (**www.nift.ac.in**)
6. Indian Institute of Information Technology, Chennai (**www.iiitt.ac.in**)
7. TN National Law University, Trichy (**www.tnnlu.ac.in**)
8. National Food technology Institute (**www.niftem-t-ac.in**)
9. Handloom Institute, Salem (**www.iihtsalem.edu.in**)
10. Indian Institiute for Design(IITDM)(**www.iiitm.ac.in**)
11. Maritime University (**www.imu.edu.in**)
12. Gandhigram University (**www.ruraluniv.ac.in**)

10b) <u>UG COURSES</u>

<u>MEDICINE</u>
MBBS, BDS, NURSING, PHARMA, AYUSH (AYURVEDA,UNANI,SIDHA,HOMEOPATHY),PHYSIOTHERAY,OCCUPATIONAL THERAPY, AUDIOLOGY, OPTOMETRY, RADIO THERAPY, SPEECH THERAPHY, MEDICAL LAB TECHNOLOGY, BVSc (FOOD, DAIRY, POULTRY)

<u>AGRICULTURE</u>
BSc - (AGRI,HORTICULTURE,FORESTRY)
BE - (AGRI ENGINEERING)
BTech-(FOOD NUTRITION AND DIETICIAN; SERVICULTURE, FOOD TECHNOLOGY, BIOTECH, ENERGY & ENVIRONMENTAL ENGINEERING), AGRI & IRRIGATION ENGG

AGRI BUSINESS MANAGEMENT

FISHERIES

BFC - FISHERIES SCIENCE

BTECH - FISHERIES ENGINEERING, BIOTECH, FISHERIES & NAUTICAL TECHNOLOGY, ENERGY & ENVIRONMENT ENGG FISHERIES BUSINESS MANAGEMENT

BVoc - INDIUSTRIAL FISH PROCESSING, INDUSTRIAL FISHING TECHNOLOGY, AQUATIC ANIMAL HEALTH MANAGEMENT

ENGINEERING

Civil, Architecture, Naval Architecture, Mechanical, Automobile, Aeronautical, Electronics & Communication (ECE), Electrical & Electronics Engineering (EEE), Electronics & Instrumentation (EIE),It, Computer Science, Nano Engineering, Production, Industrial Engineering, Marine Engineering, Mechatronics, Metallurgy, Textile, Material Science & Engg. Mining, Cyber Security, Data Science, Artificial Intelligence & Machine Learning, Robotics And Automation Engg, Internet Of Things, Biotech, Chemical, Biomedical, Petroleum Refining & Petrochemicals, Rubber & Plastics, Ceramics, Leather, Environmental Engg. Pharma Technology, Food Technology, Geo Informatics, Printing Technology Etc.

ACCOUNT AND RELATED

BCOM. BCOM CA, BCOM PA, BCA, CHARTERED ACCOUNTANCY (CA), COST ACCOUNTING (ICWA), COMPANY SECRETARY (CS), HARTERED FINANCIAL ANALYSTS (CFA)

MANAGEMENT, MATHS & ARTS RELATED

BBM, BA (CORPORATE SECRETARSHIP) BSW, BBA, BSc(MATHS), BSc (STATISTICS)

SCIENCE RELATED

Bsc - Chemistry, Phyics, Botany, Zoology, Biochemistry, Microbiology,Cell Biology, Ecology, Molecular Biology, Physiology, Neuro Sciences, Marine Biology, Geology, Human Biology, Genetics, Biomedical Sciences, Applied Physics, Geo Physics, Material Science, Environmental Science

LAW

BA BL, BA BL (HONS), BBA LLB, BBA LLB (HONS), BCA LLB (HONS)

SANDWICH ENGINEERING COURSES

IT IS A 5 YEAR COURSE

AIR HOSTESS COURSES

GRADUATION AND TRAINING

PILOT COURSES

DEGREE WITH 3 STAGES OF TRAINING
AIR REGULATION, AIR NAVIGATION METEOROLOGY
PCL -COMMERCIAL PILOT TRAINING

11a) <u>REFERENCES</u>

<u>FOR ENGINEERING</u> - Refer

NPTEL, ASME.ORG, Engineer Explained, Physics Forum, Engineer Handbook, IEEE Journals

<u>FOR IT</u> - Refer

MIT Open University	GIT HUB
Codecademy	W3 School
Standford - Engineering Everywhere	

<u>MEDICAL</u> - Refer

Medscape	Epocrates
Brainscape	Prognosis
Online MedEd	Student Doctor Network
Osmosis	Diseases Dictionary Medical

<u>IAS</u> - Refer

clearias.com

cleariasexam.com

iasbaba.com   gktoday.in

insightonindia.com   Mrunal.org

iasparliament.com

11b) <u>OTHER IMPORTANT WEBSITES FOR JOBS</u>

1. https://civilservicecoaching.com
2. www.tnvelaivaaippu.gov.in
3. www.tamilnaducareerservices.tn.gov.in
4. www.tnskill.tn.gov.in
5. www.mhrdnats.gov.in (Apprentice Ship Scheme)

www.ingramcontent.com/pod-product-compliance
Lightning Source LLC
LaVergne TN
LVHW041435170726
843492LV00008B/2618